ALSO BY CLAUDETTE FRANCIS

THE MYSTERY OF THE RESURRECTION

AN INSPIRATIONAL DRAMA ON THE RESURRECTION OF JESUS CHRIST

…WITH TESTIMONIES FROM HIGH-PROFILE STAR WITNESSES

Jesus Is Risen

An Easter Play For Children

Claudette Francis

authorHOUSE

AuthorHouse™
1663 Liberty Drive
Bloomington, IN 47403
www.authorhouse.com
Phone: 833-262-8899

Published by AuthorHouse   04/08/2021

ISBN: 978-1-4389-8103-1 (sc)
ISBN: 978-1-4490-4898-3 (e)

4 Sergio Marchi Street
Toronto, Ontario, Canada.M3L OB6
Email: swancletus28@gmail.com
Front Cover Design By: C. DHOUNTAL

NOTE ABOUT THIS BOOK

The information in this book is a combination of fact and fiction. The author used imagination and the Biblical story of the Resurrection to create this Spiritual fiction. No responsibility is therefore assumed for any problems arising from decisions taken by readers, based on their interpretation of issues and events contained in the book.

COVER IMAGE

The image of an Easter Egg was specially chosen, because it symbolizes rebirth for all humankind. It also symbolizes new life brought about by the Resurrection of Jesus.

DEDICATION

To children all over the world

You teach me to be patient in difficult times.
You help inspire me to pour my love
into my gift of teaching.

You show me by your hunger for God
that seeking first His Kingdom, is indeed
the essential part of my life.

Most importantly, you teach me to respect
each of you with dignity and love, because
you are all children of the one true God.

TABLE OF CONTENTS

SCENES

CAST OF CHARACTERS

Narrators 1 and 2

Judge Arnold

Bailiff

Mary Magdalene

Simon Peter, Apostle

Andrew, brother of Simon Peter, Apostle

James, son of Zebedee, Apostle

John, brother of James, Apostle

Philip, Apostle

Bartholomew, Apostle

Matthew, the tax collector, Apostle

James, son of Alphaeus, Apostle

Thaddaeus, Apostle

Simon, the Zealot, Apostle

A soldier from the Temple Guard

Cleopas

Bartimaeus

Children

The Widow of Nain and her son

Thomas, Apostle

The Jury

Jesus

NOTE FOR THE DIRECTOR

JESUS IS RISEN is a play created for children to act out at Easter time. It is written for ages 9 to 12 and is certain to delight children since it is age-appropriate and contains language that is easy to understand and deliver orally.

With a younger group, the director may opt to choose just three or four scenes for the children to perform. Performing the entire play can be reserved for older children. In the latter case, an intermission is appropriate if circumstances allow it. Whether the production is large or small, the drama will fulfill its purpose of proclaiming the message of the Resurrection of Jesus.

Clear, audible voices are vital to the play's success on stage. As such, the director should take great care in encouraging the children to speak up and project their voices while performing. This will go a long way in helping the audience follow the story.

To be effective, the cast should wear the colourful dress found in Middle Eastern cultures. Artisans can be enlisted to create costumes for the cast, and paint some of the important sceneries. Colourful backdrops will create and set the right tone for the drama.

Any stage can be transformed into a court room, equipped with a jury box, a judge's bench, and a witness box. Stage direction is purposely restrained to allow for creative interpretation of the director and abilities of the children.

Claudette Francis

Toronto, Canada

INTRODUCTION:
FROM THE TREE TO THE TOMB

Judge Arnold's courtroom

[Twelve jurors enter silently, and take their places.]

[Enter Narrators 1 and 2.]

Narrator 1:   Even though they found no cause for a sentence of death, they asked Pilate to have him [Jesus] killed. When they had carried out everything that was written about him, they took him down from the tree. *(Acts 13: 28-29)*

Narrator 2:   Now there was a garden in the place where Jesus was crucified, and in the garden there was a new tomb in which no one had ever been laid. And so because it was the day of preparation, and the tomb was nearby, they laid Jesus there. *(John 19: 41-42)*

Narrator 1:   But we bring you the Good News! God raised him from the dead.

Narrator 2:   For many days he appeared to those who came up with him from Galilee to Jerusalem, and they are now his witnesses to the people. *(Acts 13: 30-31)*

[Exit Narrators 1 and 2]

SCENE 1:
MARY MAGDALENE

[Enter Judge Arnold, who takes his seat on the bench]

Bailiff: This court is in session, Judge Arnold presiding.

Judge: Bailiff, what is the charge?

Bailiff: Your Honour, Mary Magdalene is accused of bearing false witness. She is making a false claim about Jesus, the one who was crucified, died and buried. She claims that Jesus rose from the dead, and is still alive.

Your Honour, the officials at the Synagogue want you to question Mary Magdalene and any others who believe in the resurrection of Jesus, to find out the truth.

Here are the two questions they want answered:

#1: Is Jesus risen from the dead?

#2: Is Mary Magdalene bearing false witness?

Judge: Very well, call the first witness.

Bailiff: *[in a loud voice]* Mary Magdalene!

[Enter Mary Magdalene]

Judge: What is your name, and where do you live?

Mary Magdalene: My name is Mary Magdalene, and I live in Galilee.

Judge: Do you know the man, Jesus?

Mary Magdalene: Yes, he is the Messiah sent by God.

Judge: The charge against you is bearing false witness. You are spreading lies about this Jesus. You say that this Jesus who was crucified, who died and was buried, rose from the dead, and is still alive among us today? Mary Magdalene, how do you plead to the charge of bearing false witness?

Mary Magdalene: Not guilty, Your Honour.

Judge: Did you witness Jesus' crucifixion, death and burial?

Mary Magdalene: Yes, Your Honour.

Judge: Where was he buried?

Mary Magdalene: He was buried in Joseph's tomb.

Judge: Did you visit the tomb early on Sunday morning?

Mary Magdalene: Yes, Your Honour, I did.

Judge: Why did you go there?

Mary Magdalene: I went there to see the tomb. *(Matthew 28:1)*

Judge: Tell this court what happened when you arrived there.

Mary Magdalene: *[proudly]* Your Honour, I came to the tomb and saw that the stone was removed, so I ran to find Simon Peter and the other apostle, the one whom Jesus loved, to tell them what had happened. *(John 20:1)*

Judge:	Did you find them?
Mary Magdalene:	Yes, Your Honour. I told them the bad news and they hurried over to the tomb to see for themselves.
Judge:	What did they find?
Mary Magdalene:	They found everything just as I had told them. They entered the tomb and found that Jesus' body was not there.
Judge:	What do you suppose happened to the body, Mary Magdalene?
Mary Magdalene:	It resurrected!
Judge:	*[in shock]* RES-UR-RECT-ED? What do you mean?
Mary Magdalene:	I mean... *[Pause]* Jesus came out of the tomb alive!
Judge:	Did Jesus ever speak about his resurrection?
Mary Magdalene:	Yes, Your Honour. He spoke about his resurrection many times, but no one understood what he meant.
Judge:	Do you really believe this resurrection story, Mary Magdalene?
Mary Magdalene:	Yes, Your Honour, with all my heart. I do believe it. This is what the resurrection of Jesus is all about. To the unbeliever, it is nothing but nonsense; but to us, his followers, it is the Good News of salvation.
Judge:	*[frustrated]* Mary Magdalene, you may go. Bailiff, call the next witness.

[Exit Mary Magdalene]

SCENE 2:
SIMON PETER

Bailiff: Simon Peter!

[Enter Simon Peter]

Judge: Do you know the man, Jesus?

Simon Peter: Yes, Your Honour. I am one of his apostles.

Judge: Tell this court what you know about the resurrection of Jesus.

Simon Peter: Early on Sunday morning, Mary Magdalene came to see the apostle, John and me. She said that she had some very bad news for us.

Judge: Tell us what the bad news was about.

Simon Peter: Your Honour, she said, "They have taken the Lord out of the tomb, and we do not know where they have laid him." *(John 20:2)*

Judge: How did you react to such bad news?

Simon Peter: I was shocked, but I decided to go and investigate the matter, so John and I set out and went toward the tomb. John, being younger and stronger outran me, and reached the tomb first.

He bent down to look in and saw the linen wrappings lying there, but he did not go in. (John 20:3-6) Then I arrived, and I went into the tomb.

Judge:	Continue, Simon Peter. What did you see?

Simon Peter: I saw the linen wrappings lying there and the cloth that had been on Jesus' head, not lying with the linen wrappings, but rolled up in a place by itself. *(John 20: 6-7)*

Judge: What became of your friend, John?

Simon Peter: *[Pause] H*e also went in and he saw and believed. *(John 20:8)*

Judge: While Jesus was with you, did he tell you he would rise from the dead?

Simon Peter: Yes, Your Honour, on many occasions, *[Pause]* but I did not understand what he meant.

Judge: Is that all, Simon Peter?

Simon Peter: No, Your Honour. Later that same day, Mary Magdalene returned and announced that she had seen the Lord, and he had said things to her. *(John 20: 18)*

Judge: She did, did she? Bailiff, summon Mary Magdalene back to court.

Bailiff: Yes, Your Honour.

Judge: Simon Peter, you may go.

[Exit Simon Peter]

SCENE 3:
MARY MAGDALENE RETURNS

[Enter Mary Magdalene]

Judge: Mary Magdalene, Simon Peter testified that you actually saw the risen Jesus. Is that true?

Mary Magdalene: Yes, Your Honour. I did. I saw the risen Jesus, just as clearly as I am seeing you now.

Judge: Mary Magdalene, let me remind you that you are under oath.

Mary Magdalene: Thank you, Your Honour, but I know what I saw, and I am telling the truth, the whole truth, and nothing but the truth.

Judge: Tell this court where and when you saw the risen Jesus.

Mary Magdalene: I returned to the tomb and stood weeping outside. As I wept, I bent over to look into the tomb and I saw two angels in white, sitting where the body of Jesus had been lying, one at the head and one at the feet. *(John 20:11-12)*

Judge: Did they say anything to you?

Mary Magdalene: Yes, Your Honour. They asked, "Woman, why are you weeping?" *(John 20:13)*

Judge:	How did you answer?
Mary Magdalene:	I said, "They had taken away my Lord, and I did not know where they had laid him." *(John 20:13)*
Judge:	Did you ever find him?
Mary Magdalene:	Yes, Your Honour. I turned around and saw Jesus standing there, but I did not know that it was Jesus. *(John 20:14)*
Judge:	What did he say?
Mary Magdalene:	He said, "Woman, why are you weeping? Who are you looking for?" You see, Your Honour, I thought that I had seen the gardener, so I said to him, "Sir, if you have carried him away, tell me where you have laid him, and I will take him away." *(John 20: 15)*
Judge:	What a strange story! What happened next?
Mary Magdalene:	He said, "Mary!" I turned and said to him in Hebrew, "Rabbouni!" That means Teacher, Your Honour.*(John 20:16)*
Judge:	I know what Rabbouni means, Mary Magdalene. Continue with your testimony.
Mary Magdalene:	I am sorry, Your Honour. Then Jesus said to me, "Do not hold on to me, because I have not yet ascended to the Father. But go to my brothers and say to them, 'I am ascending to my Father and your Father, to my God and your God.' " *(John 20:17)*
Judge:	Did you deliver the message?

Mary Magdalene: Yes, Your Honour. I went and announced to the apostles that
                    I had seen the Lord and related to them what he had told me.
                    (John 20:18)

Judge: Did anyone else actually see this risen Jesus?

Mary Magdalene: Yes, Your Honour. His apostles saw him, too.

Judge: Mary Magdalene, you may go. Bailiff, summon Jesus' apostles
                    next.

[Exit Mary Magdalene]

SCENE 4:
ANDREW SPEAKS FOR THE APOSTLES

Bailiff: Apostles of Jesus!

[Enter nine of Jesus' Apostles: Andrew, James, son of Zebedee, John, Philip, Bartholomew, Matthew, James, son of Alphaeus, Thaddaeus, and Simon, the Zealot.]

Judge: Are you apostles of Jesus?

Apostles: *[boldly]* Yes, we are, Your Honour.

Judge: Tell this court what you know about Jesus.

[All of the apostles begin to give their testimonies at the same time.]

Judge: *[interrupting]* ORDER! ORDER! ORDER! *[hits his gavel once on the desk, and shouts.]* From now on, only one of you will do the talking in this courtroom.

[The judge picks up, from his desk, a sheet of paper on which is listed, in alphabetical order, all the names of the witnesses. He then chooses one name from his list and declares.] Andrew, you may speak for the apostles. Give this court your testimony.

[Andrew takes a step forward]

Andrew: It was evening on the first day of the week, and the doors of the house were locked for fear of the people, Jesus came and stood among us and said, "Peace be with you!" After he said this, he showed us his hands and his side. (John 20:19-20)

Judge: How did you react?

Andrew: *[passionately]* We rejoiced when we saw the Lord. Jesus said to us again, "Peace be with you! As the Father has sent me, so I send you." *(John 20:21)*

Judge: Is that all?

Andrew: No, Your Honour. Then he breathed on us and said, "Receive the Holy Spirit. If you forgive the sins of any, they are forgiven them; if you retain the sins of any, they are retained." *(John 20: 22-23)*

Judge: Is that the whole story, Andrew?

Andrew: [*Proudly]* Yes, Your Honour, but if I may, I would like to say that this is what *JESUS IS RISEN* is all about. *[Pause]* It is truly the Good News of salvation.

Judge: *[puzzled]* Andrew, you may go, and take the other apostles with you. Bailiff, call the next witness.

[Exit Andrew and the other apostles]

SCENE 5:
A SOLDIER FROM THE TEMPLE GUARD

Bailiff: Soldier from the Temple Guard!

[Enter Soldier]

Judge: What is your name?

Guardin: *[proudly]* Guardin, Your Honour, Soldier G0012, Temple Guard Services!

Judge: Tell this court what took place on the Friday that Jesus died and was buried.

Guardin: Your Honour, some soldiers from the Temple Guard, including myself among them, were told to go and secure Jesus' tomb and keep watch over it.

Judge: *[confused] I* see, but why were the Temple authorities so concerned about securing Jesus' tomb?

Guardin: Your Honour, after Jesus died, and was buried, the chief priests and the Pharisees gathered before Pilate and reminded him about what Jesus had said while he was still alive… "After three days I will rise again." Then they requested that the tomb be made secure until the third day; otherwise the disciples may go and steal him away. *(Matthew 27: 62-64)*

Judge: How did Pilate respond to their request?

Guardin: He said, "You have a guard of soldiers; go, make it as secure as you can." That is how the Temple Guard became involved with guarding the tomb.

Judge: Is that the end of your testimony, Guardin?

Guardin: *[rolling his eyes]* No, Your Honour. The chief priests and the Pharisees gave us our orders, and there we were out there in the dark night fulfilling our duty!

Judge: *[puzzled]* Were you expecting anything strange to happen?

Guardin: *[reluctantly]* No, Your Honour.

Judge: *[puzzled]* How could that be? Did you not hear the news?

Guardin: *[confidently]* Yes, Your Honour, we heard rumours, but certainly that could not be true. You have to believe that such news is pure nonsense. We would have been the very first ones to see him if indeed he did come out of the tomb. Wouldn't you agree with me, Your Honour?

Judge: Guardin, I ask the questions in this courtroom! You continue with your testimony.

Guardin: Yes, Your Honour. We woke up the next morning and everything seemed normal to us. Then the chief priests and the elders came to us and offered us a large sum of money if we would keep our mouths shut about what may or may not have happened during the night. (Matthew 28:12)

Judge: *[amazed]* Is this the end of your testimony, Guardin?

Guardin: No, Your Honour. They also told us to say that his disciples came by night and stole him away, while we were asleep. *(Matthew 28:13)* We are not the bad guys, Your Honour! We were only following orders. We did our job and we were paid for it.

Judge: I see. Go on with your testimony.

Guardin: To this day we, the Soldiers of the Temple Guard, still believe that that is what really happened. There was no resurrection, Your Honour. Jesus' disciples stole his body from the tomb while we were asleep. This is our report and we stand by it!

Judge: Guardin, you may go. Bailiff, call the next witness.

[Exit Guardin]

SCENE 6:
ON THE ROAD TO EMMAUS

Bailiff;   Cleopas!

[Enter Cleopas]

Judge: Cleopas, Mary Magdalene and others testified that Jesus of Nazareth resurrected from the dead. Have you any proof that this mysterious event actually happened?

Cleopas: *[with confidence]* Yes, Your Honour. I saw the resurrected Jesus with my own eyes.

Judge: Relate the circumstances as they occurred.

Cleopas: Your Honour, three days after Jesus was buried, two of us were going from Jerusalem to a village called Emmaus and we were talking with each other about all the things that had happened. While we were talking and discussing, Jesus himself came near and went with us but our eyes were kept from recognizing him. *(Luke 24:13-16)*

Judge: How interesting! How different was he from the Jesus you knew?

Cleopas: Your Honour, he was very different, and so we regarded him as just another stranger, but then, he asked us, "What are you discussing with each other while you walk along?" At that, Your Honour, we stood still, looking sad. *(Luke 24:17)*

Judge:	*[bewildered]* Why were you sad?
Cleopas:	Your Honour, we could not believe that he had not heard the news, so we asked him a question.
Judge:	What was your question?
Cleopas:	I asked him, "Are you the only stranger in Jerusalem who does not know the things that have taken place there in these days?" *(Luke 24:18)*
Judge:	What was his reply?
Cleopas:	*[embarrassed]* Your Honour, he replied, "What things?" We found it strange that he appeared not to have a clue about what we were saying, so we replied, "The things about Jesus of Nazareth, who was a prophet mighty in deed and word before God and all the people and how our chief priests and leaders handed him over to be condemned to death and crucified him." *(Luke 24: 19-20)*
Judge:	Was he surprised to hear your news?
Cleopas:	No, Your Honour. [Pause] He went on to tell us all about the Messiah. Beginning with Moses and all the prophets, he interpreted to us the things about himself in all the scripture. Even after that, we still did not know that he was talking about himself.
Judge:	*[astonished]* That must have frustrated you!
Cleopas:	Certainly, Your Honour. You see, we had hoped that the Messiah was the one to redeem Israel. *(Luke 24:21)* We did not expect the Messiah to be condemned to death and crucified. However, the stranger told us that it was necessary that the Messiah should suffer these things and then enter into his glory. *(Luke 24:26)*
Judge:	Did that make any sense to you?

Cleopas:	Not very much, Your Honour, but as we came near the village to which we were going, he walked ahead as if he were going on, but we urged him strongly saying, "Stay with us, because it is almost evening and the day is now nearly over." *(Luke 24:28-29)*
Judge:	Did he stay?
Cleopas:	Yes, Your Honour. He came in and when he was at the table with us, he took bread, blessed it and broke it, and gave it to us. Then our eyes were opened, and we recognized that the stranger was Jesus himself; and he vanished from our sight. *(Luke 24: 30-31)*
Judge:	That is incredible! What a surprise that must have been for you and your companion!
Cleopas:	Your Honour, that same hour, we got up and returned to Jerusalem; and we found the eleven apostles and their companions gathered together. They were saying, "The Lord has risen indeed, and he has appeared to Simon!" *(Luke 24:33-34)* We told them all that had happened to us, and how Jesus appeared to us, too.
Judge:	*[looking skeptical]* Did they believe your story?
Cleopas:	*[confident]* Yes, Your Honour, without a doubt.
Judge:	Thank you, Cleopas, you may go!

[Exit Cleopas]

Judge:	Bailiff, this court will be in recess for fifteen minutes.
Bailiff:	*[to everyone in the courtroom]* This court will be in recess for fifteen minutes. All rise!

[Exit Judge Arnold and his court officials]

SCENE 7:
FLASHBACK

[While Judge Arnold and his court officials are out of his courtroom, an intruder, Bartimaeus, gives out a loud cry at the entrance of the courtroom, then comes into the courtroom dressed in his blind man's cloak, and faces the audience.]

Bartimaeus: I used to sit by the roadside, begging. Then one day I heard that Jesus was passing by. I shouted, "Jesus, Son of David, have mercy on me!" Jesus called me. I threw off my cloak and ran to him. *[Bartimaeus throws off his cloak unto the floor, and continues speaking.]*

Jesus asked me, "What do you want me to do for you?" I replied, "Lord, let me see again." Then Jesus said to me, "Receive your sight; your faith has saved you." Immediately I regained my sight and followed him, glorifying God; and all the people, when they saw it, praised God. *(Luke 18: 35- 43)*

[Bartimaeus leaves his cloak where it had fallen and goes to the far corner of the courtroom.]

[Enter a number of children]

Children: *[smiling]* Little children were being brought to Jesus in order that he might lay his hands on them and pray. The disciples spoke sternly to those who brought them; but Jesus said,

One child: "Let the little children come to me, and do not stop them; for it is to such as these that the kingdom of heaven belongs."

Children: And he laid his hands on them and went on his way. *(Matthew 19:13-15)*

[The children join Bartimaeus at the far corner of the courtroom.]

[Enter the widow of Nain and her son]

Widow: I am the widow from Nain, and this is my son, my only son. Once he died, and I was very distraught. As we were carrying his body out, Jesus approached the gate of the town, and he saw what was going on. He saw me crying, and he said to me, "Do not weep." Then he came forward and touched the bier, and the bearers stood still. And he said, "Young man I say to you, rise!" My dead son sat up and began to speak, and Jesus gave him back to me. Fear seized everyone; and they glorified God, saying, "A great prophet has risen among us!" and "God has looked favourably on his people!" *(Luke 7: 11-16)*

[Enter Judge Arnold and his court officials. The Judge surveys the room and is taken back by what he witnesses.]

Judge: *[angry and shaken]* Wait a minute! *[loud voice]* EXCUSE ME, PLEASE!*[Pause.]* Who invited you here? What do you think you are doing? Who are you, to come in here and carry on your own trial?

[at the judge's outburst, the widow of Nain embraces her son.

Bartimaeus, the children, the widow of Nain and her son, speak out in unison.]

All: Your Honour, we are friends of Jesus Christ of Nazareth, and we are here today to tell everyone about his good deeds.

Judge: *[irritated]* Bailiff! *[loud voice]* BAI-LIFF! *[Pause]* Where are you?

Bailiff: *[steps forward, bewildered]* Here I am, Your Honour!

Judge:	*[furious]* Who are these people? *[loud voice]* GET THEM OUT OF MY COURTROOM AT ONCE! Clear this courtroom of these intruders, immediately!
Bailiff:	Yes, Your Honour. *[the Bailiff turns to the intruders and pleads with them to leave the courtroom]* All of you, get out of here immediately, or you could end up serving the rest of your lives in prison! *[loud voice]* GET OUT AT ONCE!

[Bartimaeus and the others exit the courtroom hastily. The Bailiff snatches up Bartimaeus' cloak and throws it angrily behind them.]

Judge:	*[sighs]* Thank You. Now back to the business of this court. Bailiff, call the next witness.

SCENE 8:
THOMAS

Bailiff: Thomas!

[Enter Thomas]

Judge: What is your name?

Thomas: My name is Thomas, but many of my friends call me Doubting Thomas. Others call me Thomas, the Twin, and yet others call me Didymus.

Judge: Is that so? For the record, let it be known that in this courtroom you will be called Thomas. Period. Where were you on the night when Jesus first appeared to the apostles?

Thomas: I was asleep at home, Your Honour.

Judge: Asleep? Well, then how did you hear the news?

Thomas: The apostles told me about it, later.

Judge: What did they actually tell you?

Thomas: They said, "We have seen the Lord."

Judge: Did you believe them?

Thomas:	*[sarcastically]* Certainly not! My response to them was, "I do not believe you! Okay? Unless I see the mark of the nails in his hands, and put my finger in the mark of the nails and my hand in his side, I will not believe."
	(John 20:25) Then I left the house.
Judge:	What caused you to change from doubter to believer?
Thomas:	Your Honour, a week later Jesus' apostles were again in the house, and this time I was with them. Although the doors were shut, Jesus came and stood among us and said, "Peace be with you." *(John 20:26)*
Judge:	*[leans forward to Thomas]* Did he speak to you, Thomas?
Thomas:	Yes, Your Honour. He said, "Put your finger here and see my hands. Reach out your hand and put it in my side. Do not doubt but believe." *(John 20:27)*
Judge:	What happened next?
Thomas:	Your Honour, I answered him, "My Lord and my God!"*(John 20:28)*
Judge:	What was his response?
Thomas:	Your Honour, Jesus rebuked me. He said, "Have you believed because you have seen me? Blessed are those who have not seen and yet have come to believe."*(John 20 29)*
Judge:	So I guess it is fair to say that that is the moment when you changed from doubter to believer.
Thomas:	*[confidently]* Certainly, Your Honour, and I will always remain a believer.
Judge:	Is that all, Thomas?

Thomas: Yes, Your Honour, but I would like to add this. We have given our testimonies and our testimonies are true. You must believe that Jesus is the Messiah, the Son of God, and that through believing you may have life in his name. *(John 20:31)*

Judge: Well, Thomas, you impressed me with your testimony! Thank you. You may go.

[Exit Thomas]

Judge: *[to the jury]* Ladies and Gentlemen of the jury, you have heard the evidence from several witnesses. To summarize, Mary Magdalene testifies that she found an empty tomb, so she believes Jesus rose from the dead. Peter and John agree with her testimony.

Guardin doubts the resurrection ever took place. Then there are other witnesses who testified that they actually saw the risen Jesus. Now as jurors, this is your time to find the truth. You have a civic duty to do the right thing. Let me remind you about the two questions you will deliberate.

#1: Is Jesus risen from the dead?

#2: Is Mary Magdalene bearing false witness?

Consider well all the evidence presented at this trial and reach a just decision. This court awaits your verdict. *[To the Bailiff]* This court is adjourned until further notice.

Bailiff: This court is adjourned until further notice. All rise!

[Judge Arnold leaves the courtroom, members of the jury retire to the jury room, and everyone else leaves the court room to await the jury's decision.]

SCENE 9:
THE VERDICT IS IN

[Enter Judge Arnold]

Judge: Members of the Jury, have you reached a verdict?

Foreperson: Yes, Your Honour, we have reached a verdict.

Judge: Present your verdict to the Bailiff.

[The bailiff walks over to the foreperson of the jury and receives a paper. He then walks back to Judge Arnold and presents the paper to him. The bailiff returns to his position.]

Judge: *[reads the verdict, silently to himself.]* Foreperson of the jury, is your verdict unanimous?

Foreperson: Yes, Your Honour, our verdict is unanimous.

Judge: Tell this court your findings.

Foreperson: To Question #1: Is Jesus risen from the dead? We the jury find Jesus is indeed risen from the dead. Furthermore, we know that Jesus being raised from the dead, will never die again; death no longer has any power over him. (Romans 6:9)

[loud cheers are heard throughout the courtroom.]

To Question # 2: Is Mary Magdalene bearing false witness? We the jury find Mary Magdalene innocent of the charge of bearing false witness.

[for the second time, loud cheers erupt in the courtroom, but Guardin walks out , protesting the verdict. Outside of the courtroom, a court reporter tries to question him, but Guardin is not happy at all.]

Guardin: *[to the reporter]* Unbelievable! They accept Mary Magdalene's testimony and reject mine. They believe a man can come back from the dead? It makes no sense at all. What next? Will he come to judge the living and the dead? I stand by my story. There was no resurrection!

[Guardian walks away fuming.]

[Meanwhile in the courtroom, Judge Arnold gets ready to address the court. The eyes of all in the courtroom are fixed upon him. Everyone listens attentively.]

Bailiff: All rise!

Judge: [Rises] This is by far the most interesting case I have ever tried. You have convinced me that Jesus of Nazareth is risen from the dead. I believe your story, and will certainly pass on the good news to the officials at the Synagogue. Go in peace to love and serve your Jesus. He is truly a remarkable person. *[Pause]*

This case is DISMISSED! *[the judge hits his gavel once.]*

Mary Magdalene, you are free to go.

[APPLAUSE]

SCENE 10:
THE GRAND FINALE

[Enter Jesus]

[Seeing Jesus enter, Judge Arnold stands up in awe.]

Jesus: Peace be with you.

[The rest of the courtroom turns to face Jesus.]

Jesus: You have been very courageous in bearing witness to my resurrection. I now commission you to go out and tell the good news everywhere. Do not be frightened or dismayed for the LORD your God is with you wherever you go. *(Joshua 1:9)*

As the Father has sent me, so I send you. Go and make the world a better place! In everything, do to others as you would have them do to you,... *(Matthew 7:12)*

I give you a new commandment, that you love one another. Just as I have loved you, you also should love one another. By this everyone will know that you are my disciples, if you have love for one another. *(John 13:34-35)*

Be kind to one another, tenderhearted, forgiving one another, as God in Christ has forgiven you. Therefore be imitators of God, as beloved children, and live in love, as I loved you. *(Ephesians 4: 32:5:1)*

Peace I leave with you; my peace I give to you. Rise, let us be on our way. *(John 14:27,31)*

CONCLUSION

What a wonderful time of the year Easter is! It is a time for Easter parades, family picnics, and Easter egg hunts. It is also a time when baby ducklings, lambs, chicks and other young animals arrive on farms, at Zoos, and in Shopping Malls. How very delightful this time of year is for children!

Easter is also a time for peace and thanksgiving. Great numbers of Christians attend church services to hear the wonderful story of Jesus' resurrection, and to reflect on its sign of new life for all. What a privilege it is for Christians to carry the Resurrection message of peace, hope, and joy to others!

Many of Jesus' followers saw him after his resurrection. Mary Magdalene hurried to tell Peter what she saw at the tomb. The Apostles told Thomas what they saw, and the disciples from Emmaus hurried back late at night to tell the Apostles what they saw. Although Jesus' closest followers were amazed at the story, some of them believed it, and some did not. Nevertheless, Jesus appeared to them and greeted them saying, "Peace be to you." His ascension to heaven took place forty days after his resurrection.

Author Claudette Francis presents a dramatic account of Jesus' *Resurrection* in two of her books: *JESUS IS RISEN—written for ages 9 to 12 years*, and *THE MYSTERY OF THE RESURRECTION—written for* ages 13 years and up. She wishes that children, and adults, regardless of their faith, religion or denomination (no one is excluded) will discover that this drama will capture their imagination, and increase their knowledge of a well-known and spectacular event in the Bible.

ACTIVITIES

Answer the following questions: (There is one question for each scene.)

1. Which of the following words best describe Mary Magdalene?

   loyal   boring   disciple   faithful

2. Where did Simon Peter and John go after hearing the bad news from Mary Magdalene?

3. Who was the first person to see the risen Jesus?

4. Which of the following words best describe the soldier?

   brave   cruel   hard-working   curious

5. Describe the reaction of the apostles when they saw the risen Jesus.

6. When did Cleopas and his companion recognize Jesus?

7. Why were the friends of Jesus Christ of Nazareth in the courtroom?

8. Who said these words? "My Lord and my God!"

9. After reading the verdict, do you think the jurors were just?

10. Which of the following statements show a good understanding of Jesus' new commandment?

    a. You and your friends invite a new student to join in your games.
    b. You forgive your friend who hurt your feelings.
    c. You and your friends prepare gift boxes to send to children who have less than you.

DRAWING

Draw the part of the drama that you like best.

DRAWING

Draw your favourite character from this drama.

JESUS IS RISEN WORD FIND

G	A	J	B	C	H	L	O	V	E	A	V	X	O	C
O	D	F	E	K	O	M	P	Q	C	U	W	Y	M	D
D	G	H	J	S	L	R	S	T	A	B	Z	C	L	J
H	M	N	P	U	Y	W	X	Y	E	C	F	G	K	O
T	O	M	B	C	S	C	R	I	P	T	U	R	E	S
E	D	A	G	H	P	R	M	L	N	O	P	Q	U	E
R	B	R	R	C	I	U	S	M	G	B	C	S	A	P
A	L	Y	T	H	R	C	L	D	D	D	E	R	B	H
Z	A	C	H	I	I	I	B	I	I	J	N	L	N	V
A	N	M	O	E	T	F	N	S	V	P	V	A	C	S
N	B	Q	M	F	V	I	E	C	A	I	K	B	A	G
P	O	N	A	P	C	E	S	I	D	L	A	V	M	N
L	C	O	S	R	N	D	I	P	D	A	E	L	O	R
N	B	U	R	I	E	D	R	L	V	T	O	S	W	M
C	V	B	D	E	O	V	L	E	H	E	A	V	E	N
T	M	A	A	S	C	E	N	S	I	O	N	D	T	S
L	R	Q	V	T	R	E	T	E	P	N	O	M	I	S
N	A	I	T	S	I	R	H	C	T	I	B	Q	M	N
O	P	R	E	S	U	R	R	E	C	T	I	O	N	W

Find the listed words in the diagram. They go forward, backward, up, down, and diagonally.

ASCENSION	HEAVEN	PILATE	BURIED	HOLY SPIRIT	RESURRECTION
CHIEF PRIESTS	JESUS	RISEN	CHRISTIAN	JOSEPH	SAVE
CRUCIFIED	LOVE	SCRIPTURES	DAVID	MARY	SIMON PETER
DISCIPLES	NAZARETH	THOMAS	GOD	PEACE	TOMB

Printed in the United States
by Baker & Taylor Publisher Services